St Viper's Scho‹

'St Viper's is like *The I*
steroids. A fast-paced, ‹ ... ‹.‹ture.
Recommended.' Jim Carrington

'It's fast-paced, funny, full of action to keep a young reader turning the page to see if Demon is going to make it, and with lots to amuse a grown up reading aloud – not that you should read this at bed-time! (Too exciting.)' Julia Green

'Take a mixture of Super Villains from Dark Owls to Demons, add a sprinkling of Robots and Rocket Ships and you've got a recipe for a rip-roaring adventure that will keep fun-lovers entertained from seven to seventy!' Steve Voake

'As the first book from new publishing venture, Electrik Inc, *St Viper's School for Super Villains* bodes well for the company. It is ruthlessly edited, with a fine attention to detail that more than holds its own against traditional publishing houses. It is clear that the combined experience of the team behind the text has paid off.' Elen Caldecott

'A well constructed story packed with action, jokes and lots of alliterative silliness to keep young readers entertained, engaged and giggling. It's like a cracking good theme park ride. Lots of thrilling ups and downs with a promise that you can have as much fun on the sequel.' Nicola Davies

This is an Electrik Inc book.

Electrik Inc is a brand new collective combining great writing for children and young adults, sharp editing and professional independent publishing (ebooks and print on demand). With more than 50 years' industry experience between them – plus four MAs in Writing for Young People from Bath Spa University – the founders of Electrik Inc have one objective: to make each book the best it can be.

www.electrikinc.wordpress.com

ST VIPER'S SCHOOL FOR SUPER VILLAINS

THE RIOTOUS ROCKET SHIP ROBBERY

BY KIM DONOVAN
ILLUSTRATED BY PETHERICK BUTTON
SQUAWK BOOKS

Published by Squawk Books Ltd

Text copyright 2011 Kim Donovan

Illustrations copyright 2011 Petherick Button

ISBN: 978-0-9571300-0-5

FOR CHRISTOPHER

To Megan
With Wicked Wishes
Kim Donovan x

INTRODUCING:

DR SUPER EVIL

THUNDERSKULL

STRETCH

WOLFGANG

DEMON

SHRINK

LEVITATE

MR MADNESS

DARK OWL

CHILL

Trouble Ahead

Hidden inside a dark cloud, the airship flew over the shark-infested ocean towards St Viper's School for Super Villains.

In the passenger deck, pupils laughed, burped and yelled at one another, drowning out the hum of the engine. Demon Kid, one of the new First Years, sized up the other boys and girls relaxing on leather sofas or sticking their heads out of windows. They had frost on their eyebrows when they pulled their heads in. There were kids with massive muscles, wings, spiky bodies and tentacles - nothing out of the ordinary. He watched a girl squeeze a pulsating pimple in the direction of the teacher's coffee cup. A silver-skinned boy produced a crackle of zigzag lightning from the end of his finger. Demon ducked as it flashed over his head – ZZHOOM! – hit a picture frame and left a brown scorch mark behind.

I can beat that, thought Demon. *I'll show everyone what a real super villain can do – just like my dad.* He waited until he felt a burning sensation in his throat and blew a jet of red and orange flame out of his mouth. WHOOSH! A wild-haired teacher sitting nearby rubbed his ears, then rustled his copy of the *Black-Market Scientist* and flicked to an article on how to grow deadly plague germs.

Demon stopped breathing fire as none of the pupils seemed to be taking any notice of him either. He tugged on the tight neck of his new school uniform: an all-in-one acid green jumpsuit with black stripes down both sides, a belt with a snake buckle, a detachable cape and knee-high boots. He checked his watch. Had they really only been up in the air for twenty-five minutes?

'How long until we get there?' he asked a girl with a black eye mask who was relaxing on a reclining chair next to him. During take off she'd been talking non-stop to another boy with scaly lizard skin.

'I bet it'll take hours,' she replied, shaking her purple ponytail. 'The school's gotta be really far away or everyone would find it.'

'Hours!' He'd rather tear off his claws with his teeth than sit still for that long.

The girl extended one of her arms beyond its normal length and shook Demon's hand. 'My name is Stretch. Stacey Stretch.' PYYAANG! Her arm pinged back like elastic to its normal size.

'I'm -'

'No, don't tell me. I'll guess.' She looked Demon up and down. 'Spiky red hair, shiny black eyes, claws and a tail. Your name must be Devil-Boy?'

'No, it's Demon Kid. But you can call me Demon.'

An icy jab on the back of his neck made him jump. Demon glanced over his shoulder at a group of much bigger and meaner-looking kids. A blue-skinned boy with hair sculpted into a peak stuck out his pierced tongue and the others laughed.

Demon gave the big kids a hard stare and turned back. He ran a claw over the skin of his neck, scraped away something cold and crunchy and examined it. Underneath his claw a thin layer of frost glistened.

'Good one, Chill,' he heard someone say behind him.

Stretch leaned towards Demon. 'I bet Chill's the blue one,' she whispered.

Demon felt the icy touch again. This time a shot of extreme cold ran all the way down his spine to the tip of his tail.

Pressure built inside his head like an inflating balloon. He caught sight of his hands. They were turning red. His vision blurred as if a red mist had filled the cabin. *They'll be sorry in a minute.*

'Freeze him to *death*,' said one of Chill's friends.

Demon's temper flared. His hair burst into flames, fire flickered on the backs of his hands and his chair caught light. Without even thinking about it, he swivelled and a firebolt blazed from his mouth - FWOOSH! - and scorched Chill's hand.

ZSSSSS! A jet of something cold knocked Demon sideways off his chair. KERTHUMP!

Thick white foam sprayed inside his ear, down his back, up his nose and in his mouth. He sneezed and spluttered. The flames dampened down and in a few seconds fizzled out completely.

Demon's vision slowly came back into focus and the compartment lost its red glow. 'He's not even burnt,' some pupils whispered. Others laughed at him lying on the floor, covered in foam.

The teacher stood glaring at Demon, holding a fire extinguisher. He had several rows of pointed teeth like a shark. 'I am trying to read my journal,' he snapped.

'He started it!' Demon jumped to his feet, clenching his foamy hands into fists.

'Any more disturbance from either of you and I'll have you searching the toilets for bog bombs twice a day, every day for the entire school year,' said the teacher. 'Understood?'

'Yeah.' Chill rolled his eyes.

'Yes, sir,' said Demon.

The teacher sat down, propped the extinguisher between his legs and put his head back in the magazine.

Chill leaned over Demon's shoulder, holding his burnt hand in front of Demon's face. 'You're going to pay for that, little firebug.'

The Villain's Lair

'We could make 'im our slave,' said a boy with biceps like cannonballs. He eyeballed Demon.

'Hmmm, I do have a job vacancy. My last slave died of exhaustion.' Chill's mouth curled into a thin-lipped smile. 'From now on you're going to be on call for us day and night. If we say go swim with the sharks you do it.' He glanced at Stretch. 'You too, bubblegum.'

'Whoa! I didn't do anything,' said Stretch.

Demon swivelled and banged his head against the sofa cushion. It smelt disgusting, of burnt toast.

'Hey, you could have picked a fight with someone smaller,' Stretch said to him. 'We're never going to look like awesome super villains against the senior year.'

'Sorry,' he snapped.

Stretch turned away from him and went back to talking to the boy on the other side of her. She made no attempt to include Demon in the conversation.

Over the next hour Demon's skin returned to its normal shade of pink and his two hearts stopped thumping so hard. *What a rubbish first impression to make,* he thought. *And I've made trouble for Stretch.* Demon tried to catch her eye but she avoided his gaze.

'I really am sorry for dragging you into it,' he said in a low voice.

Stretch straightened up and gave Demon a small smile. 'It's okay. I like a challenge.'

The loud speaker crackled. 'We will shortly be arriving at St Viper's,' said the pilot. 'Hold on tight!'

Demon fizzed with a mix of nerves and excitement. The view outside the window had changed from dark cloud to blue sky. Below them was an island with white sand, swaying palm trees and a volcano surrounded by thick jungle.

Wisps of smoke floated out of the volcano's jagged mouth and, as they moved closer, ropes knocked against the windows. Demon dug his claws into the armrests.

The airship lowered into the crater past orangey-brown rock and dropped into a swirl of smoke.

At the front of the cabin a small girl with cobwebs in her hair screamed and the older kids burst out laughing. 'Help! We're going to be barbecued!' joked Chill.

'I'm tellin' you man, dis baby is gonna blow,' shouted his friend, trying to frighten the younger kids even more.

The smoke thinned to show the bottom of a gigantic chamber. A circular platform filled the floor like a huge coin. The end of the ropes wound around six metal drums on the platform, pulling the airship down.

'My best friend is gonna be so jealous when I tell her my school's inside a volcano,' said Stretch.

'You can't tell her about it,' replied Demon. 'The school's a secret.'

Stretch sighed. 'That's so not fair.'

BUMP! The airship landed and the thrum of the engine died. Demon retracted his claws.

'I hope you enjoyed travelling with Enemy Airlines,' said the pilot. 'Please ensure you take all your personal belongings and lethal weapons with you.'

All the pupils except Demon and Stretch jumped up straight away. They grabbed their bags, bazookas and laser blasters, then they bit and scratched and pulled each other's hair all the way to the exit.

Wow! They're as nasty as piranhas, thought Demon.

Chill stopped in front of the hatch and turned to face Demon. 'We'll be seeing you soon to give you your orders,' he said.

'In your dreams,' Demon muttered.

He and Stretch waited their turn to leave the airship, then jumped out onto the concrete landing pad. The air felt moist and warm. On Demon's right was a boy with short brown hair, a freckly nose and glasses. He could easily have been mistaken for an "ultra-ordinary" if he wasn't flying a few feet off the ground in a pair of silver boots with blue fire roaring from the soles.

'Cool boots,' said Demon.

'Thanks.' He smiled. 'My name's Shrink.'

'I'm Demon. And this is - '

Stretch lifted one leg up behind her, brought her foot over her shoulder, gave it a tug and then wrapped her leg around her neck like a scarf.

'Stretch,' said Demon.

Shrink blinked. 'That's amazing.'

'Gee, thanks.' Stretch grinned. 'My whole family's mega talented, but I'm the only one that's been in *Wicked Weekly*. Did you see the picture of me squashed inside a shoebox? Course, my face doesn't look the same when it's packed flat.'

Demon had been in *Wicked Weekly* more times than he could remember. But only because he happened to be with his dad when a journalist caught him on camera. They often tried to cut him out of the photo, so that just his elbow, claw or the tip of his tail remained.

He looked up at the volcano. The walls rose in a huge dome around him. Just a tiny patch of natural light filtered in through the opening at the top. Spotlights, windows and balconies had been built into the rock with metal staircases leading up to doorways at different levels.

'Wow,' Demon mumbled. 'This place is massive.'

'Volcanoes take years and years to grow this big,' explained Shrink. 'Some are a million years old.'

And it only takes a super villain a few months to turn it into the perfect secret lair, thought Demon.

They walked a few steps, climbed down a steel ladder and joined a group of nine other new kids who were all looking nervous.

BOOM! A cloud of green smoke appeared. Demon's tail twitched from side to side as he watched the smoke fade away.

Syndicate Of Supreme Evil

A man emerged from the cloud. He was tap dancing in a pair of gold lace-up boots with steel toecaps. He had a barrel-shaped chest, long skinny legs and grey hair styled into the shape of two horns. Little silver spikes covered his black cape and a white skull adorned his all-in-one suit. A small roll of belly hung over the metal belt around his waist.

He stopped jiggling around and looked at the waiting children. 'Welcome my young whippersnappers. Welcome indeed to St Viper's School for Super Villains. I am Mr Madness, the head teacher,' he said with an evil laugh. 'MWAHAHAHAHA.'

Demon trapped his twitchy tail between his legs. He'd never felt so nervous in his life.

'Here at St Viper's we are creating an elite team – a Syndicate of Supreme Evil, heh-heh – a force of unforgettable fear, ho-ho – a team of terrifying tricksters, har-har – to TAKE OVER THE WORLD.' He spun 360 degrees, threw the cape over his arm and held it up to his chin. 'Now then. You may be wondering why you have been chosen for a place at this house of horrendous hero haters. Well, I will tell you . . . it is a fact that many of you are the spawn of super villains – ' here he winked at Demon. 'A few of you have gained particular powers from paddling in pools of poison or experimenting with explosives. But only the most special students will be allowed to stay at the school.'

Demon glanced at his new classmates, wondering if they were more gifted than him. They certainly looked the part.

'My advice is to practise and practise your powers until they are perfect. Keep looking for ways to demonstrate to the teachers how deliciously despicable you really are,' continued Mr Madness. 'Dazzle us with your daring.'

As he listened, Demon's eyes widened. His mum and dad always thought he had what it took to be despicable. They'd put his name down for St Viper's at birth. Every night at bedtime, his dad had told him that, one day, Demon would be an even better super villain than him.

I'll make you proud of me, he thought and squared his shoulders. *I'll be top of the class here.*

'Those of you who are superbly sinful will be rewarded with *special school trips*,' Mr Madness continued. 'Several of our senior year pupils will be off on one in a few days' time.' He gave Demon a grin. 'Being beastly should be no problem with your genes.'

Demon forced a confident smile back.

*

17

The First Years were given the rest of the morning to unpack their bags and stow away weapons. In the afternoon they had their first lesson. Demon, Shrink and Stretch, with another new boy called Wolfgang, hurried off to "World Domination". Wolfgang scampered along on all fours. He had scruffy black hair with silver streaks, pointed ears and sideburns that were so long they ran under his chin and down his neck. The backs of his hands were very hairy, too. Over his jumpsuit he wore a tool belt with various chewed rulers and pens sticking out of its compartments.

Demon and the others walked along a steamy corridor carved out of the rock, passing metal doors on both sides.

Some pupils carried pens and books in their tentacles or flew on jet-powered skateboards. Demon saw kids swaggering along to their own theme tunes, which boomed out of music players clipped to their jumpsuits. It was time he had his own song. A girl with tiny cubes of polystyrene stuck on the ends of her spines looked at Demon and whispered something to her one-eyed friend. They both giggled.

I bet they're laughing at me being hosed down on the airship, Demon thought. *No one would dare laugh at my dad.*

'Okay, where next?' he asked out loud.

Shrink opened his hand to reveal a shiny gadget in his palm. It had a plan of the school on the screen. 'We go through this door and down the back stairs,' he said. 'World Domination is on the ground floor.'

They followed Shrink's directions and started down the stairs, walking in twos, with Demon and Stretch at the front and Shrink and Wolfgang behind. Only a few pupils were using this staircase.

A big eagle flew over Demon's head, its brown wings brushing the sides of the stairway. With one deft movement, it extended its talons and tugged Stretch's purple hair before swooping to the bottom of the stairs.

'Hey, I'll pluck your feathers. See how you like it!' shouted Stretch.

The shape of the bird began to blur and shift, making Demon rub his eyes. When he looked again a girl had appeared.

'Shapeshifter,' said Wolfgang. 'Ve have many in Transylvania.'

Demon glanced over his shoulder. Wolfgang had stopped and was holding his nose up in the air, sniffing. Long hairs bristled all along his neck.

Things Get Chilly

Demon followed Wolfgang's stare. There at the top of the steps stood Chill with his hands clasped behind his back. His blueish skin and bony body made him look like he'd returned from the dead. With him were the two boys and girl he'd sat with on the airship. One of the boys - the thug with bulging biceps - pulled on his fat fingers. CLICK. CLICK!

Demon's stomach did a double somersault.

'There you are, slaves.' Chill's eyes glinted dangerously. 'I want you to come to our room tonight. And wear something warm.'

Chill's sidekicks burst into laughter. 'What's da weather forecast?' asked a boy with huge golden eyes and a shaved head.

'A blast of Arctic air could see temperatures plummeting to Ice Age conditions in isolated areas.' Chill's mouth twisted into a sinister smile.

'What are you talking about?' said Shrink.

'It doesn't matter,' muttered Demon. His face felt hot and his hands reddened. 'Because we're not doing anything for them.'

'Chill, I think our new slaves need to be taught who's in charge around here,' said the girl. She had hair like a bombed bird's nest and wore an eye mask.

'I agree.' Chill's eyes turned from blue to white. FFZZZZ! Two light beams shot out of them, criss-crossed the step where Demon was standing and formed ice crystals around his feet.

'GO!' Demon shouted to the others. Stretch was already on her way down the stairs. Shrink jetted after her in his boots.

Demon spun and sprinted down the steps but the white beams lengthened and swept across the lower part of the staircase.

The steps turned white and shone with ice. His arms flailed as he tried to keep his balance.

WHUMP! He crashed onto his bottom, accidentally pulling Wolfgang over with him. They skidded across the achingly cold floor and knocked into Stretch, taking her off her feet. Then the three friends careered on down – BUMP, BUMP . . . BUMP! - landing in a tangled heap at the bottom. Demon lay on his back, sandwiched between Stretch, who had become as flat as a mat, and Wolfgang. His hairy friend breathed into his face.

Yuck! Stale dog-food breath! Demon thought. His body stung with pain.

Chill and his friends laughed.

'The party starts at 7pm. Don't be late or I'll freeze you like fish fingers,' shouted Chill.

'Ooh. Ooh. A party. I love parties!' said the muscle-bound boy. 'Bring some cake with yer.'

'Thunderskull, you oaf, it's not that sort of party,' snapped Chill. 'But come with spoons,' he said to Demon and the others.

Demon lifted his head and glared up at the older kids. His body filled with heat. Wolfgang leapt off him, growling.

'Get off me!' yelled Stretch.

Chill laughed and formed the letter "L" for loser with his thumb and finger. Then he headed for the nearest door with his cronies.

Demon tried to chase after Chill up the icy steps, but he kept slipping. Slush formed where his hot knees hit the ice. They throbbed.

Chill disappeared through the door.

Demon slumped onto the steps. Even if he'd had as many years of practise at flame-throwing and fire-breathing as Chill had with ice-making, Demon doubted whether he'd be any match for him.

Dad would have melted Chill into a puddle on the floor, he thought. *I have to start acting more like a super villain if I'm going to make a bad name for myself at this school. I'm a villain not a victim. I'll show them.*

BUZZZ! Shrink flew up beside Demon and pulled him to his feet. 'Come on, we're late for class.'

The four friends hobbled off to "World Domination". When they got there the rest of the First Years were already sitting in their leather swivel chairs, pens and paper at the ready on the black glass tabletops in front of them. The tables were arranged in the shape of a semicircle, facing an old-fashioned chalkboard. The teacher, a tall man with dark, swept-back hair and the palest skin, was busy scratching the name "Doctor Super Evil" on the board in white chalk. The sound put Demon's teeth on edge. He wore a black leather coat and clutched a cane with a gold handle shaped like a viper in his bony hand.

'You are one minute late,' he said.

World Domination

Demon, Stretch and Wolfgang limped forward. 'It's not our fault, sir,' they said together.

Shrink peered from behind Demon. 'I can show you what happened,' he said quietly. He held up his watch for Doctor Super Evil to see. 'My watch records movies. I got the whole thing.'

'Two minutes late!'

Shrink jumped.

The teacher looked down his nose at them. 'Are you late because you were trying to blow up the school?'

'No,' said Demon.

'Were you stealing the school's entire supply of sleep serum from the store cupboard?'

Demon shook his head. Then he thought: *Sleep serum. That's something I could use.*

Doctor Super Evil rolled his eyes. 'They don't even lie,' he muttered to himself. 'Well then, I'm afraid I have no choice but to give you extra homework. You will each write a two-page essay on what makes a good super villain's lair.'

'Yes, sir.' Demon sighed. First Chill wanted them to go to his room for something or other and now they had an essay to write, too! When were they ever going to have time to set booby traps for the teachers?

'Sit down!' Doctor Super Evil said.

Wolfgang squatted on the floor in front of the teacher's shiny shoes and started to chew a pencil.

'On a chair,' snapped Doctor Super Evil, pointing his cane at a group of seats.

Demon hurried over to one and sat down.

'I am Doctor Super Evil, an expert in "World Domination".' The teacher stood a little taller.

'My presence makes mighty men moan and women wail –'

Doctor Super Evil's phone rang. 'Excuse me.' He turned his back to the class. 'Hello, Mother,' he whispered. 'Yes, I have got a clean vest on. Yes, my pants are fresh, too.'

Demon, Stretch, Shrink and Wolfgang grinned at each other.

'I have to go, I'm teaching,' he said in a low voice. 'Yes, I promise I'll call you later.'

Doctor Super Evil faced the class with slightly flushed cheeks. 'First, we will do the register,' he said. 'When I call your name, you will give me the evil laugh that you will use to scare your victims.'

He picked up a list from his desk and read out: 'Hammerhead.'

'Hee, hee,' squeaked a boy who had a rectangular head and wide-set eyes.

'No, like this.' THUD! The teacher banged his cane down on the floor and threw back his head. 'HAR, HAR, HAR, HAR, HAR!' he boomed in a deep, throaty voice. 'Bella Black-Widow.'

'Heh, heh, heh,' answered the girl with cobwebs in her hair.

'You sound more like a wicked witch than a super villain. Work on it.'

He looked back down his list. 'Demon Kid.'

'HAR, HAR, HAR.'

'Not bad. Try making a grabbing movement with your claws at the same time.'

While the teacher called out everyone's name, Demon thought about what had happened on the stairs. Chill and his sidekicks would put them into cold storage unless they acted fast. The teacher had mentioned sleep serum. Putting the big kids to sleep for a few days wasn't such a mad idea. It would give him and his friends some breathing space to learn how to fight back. Demon's dad might even reward him with the eraser ray his mum had refused to let him have until his thirteenth birthday.

THUD! Doctor Super Evil rammed his cane onto the floor again bringing Demon's attention back to the lesson. The teacher paced up and down in front of his desk. 'One does not just get out of bed one morning and think, "Oh, I know. I'm going to take over the world today!" World Domination takes a lot of planning. For starters, you need a command centre from which to oversee operations and henchmen to work for you who can pack a punch. You may have to organise a jailbreak to get the right people for the job. You must have a juggernaut of explosives, a factory of firearms and a plan that details exactly how you will seize power, which you will practise, practise, practise.' He hit the floor with his cane three times.

Doctor Super Evil turned away from the class and scrawled on the blackboard, "Keep your friends close and your enemies closer."

Demon barely noticed. He was too busy thinking about what Doctor Super Evil had just said about planning. In his dad's secret study, which was reached through a door in the back of the fridge, he had a corkboard full of photos, maps and notes for his current assignment. *Dad would have a plan for putting Chill to sleep,* thought Demon. *That's what we need.*

He grabbed his special spy pen and wrote the word PLAN at the top of a fresh sheet of paper in yellow ink. The letters vanished before his eyes. He underlined what he hoped was the title, twice.

1. Steal some sleep serum.

Secret Sleep Serum

At break time, Demon and his friends stayed behind in class and sat at a table with what looked like a blank piece of paper in front of them. Demon rubbed the end of his spy pen over the page. As if by magic, several lines of untidy yellow writing appeared. Some words were written on top of other words. Different sentences merged together. And a few words had been spelled backwards.

'Vhat's zis?' asked Wolfgang, chewing on his favourite ruler.

'Our plan.' Demon frowned at the page. Only the word "cupboard" stood out.

Shrink flashed up his electronic navigation device. He tapped a finger on the screen, brought up all the school's store cupboards and began to list them. 'Weapons of Mammoth Destruction. Ultra-Ordinary Clothing and Shoe store. Forgery: Counterfeit Money, Paint-by-Number Masterpieces and Fake Passports. Mr Madness' Secret Supply of Baked Beans. The Secret Mission Store Cupboard.'

'Stop!' Stretch thumped her palms down on the desk. 'That's gotta be it. The school's only gonna need sleep serum for missions. It's not like the teachers want us falling asleep in class, right?'

'There's only one way to find out if it's in there.' Demon looked at Shrink. 'Where's the cupboard?'

Shrink tapped the screen. 'Level four,' he said.

Demon pushed back his chair and jumped to his feet. 'I don't think I'll be needing this pen again.' He held it out to Wolfgang.

'Thank you.' Wolfgang gave the pen a quick chew and then stuck it into his tool belt.

The friends left the classroom and hurried up a metal staircase. Drizzly rain fell in through the top of the volcano. It sizzled and turned to steam on the hot handrail. When they reached the fourth floor they turned down a narrow, earthy passage. Shrink buzzed along in his boots, looking at a moving red dot on the screen. He ignored several metal doors that lined the corridor and touched down in front of the last one at the end of the passage. Demon stopped next to him.

'This is it,' said Shrink.

Demon stared at a sign which read: "Secret Missions Store Cupboard". 'You'd think the teachers would have made it harder for us to find,' he said. 'This is supposed to be a school for super villains.'

But when he looked more closely, he realised there was no keyhole or handle to open the door. A square panel flashed at head height with the imprint of a hand inside it.

Wolfgang barged Demon out of the way, but Stretch got her hand into the mould first.

'I should do it because it was my idea,' said Demon.

Stretch ignored him, extending her fingers until her hand fitted perfectly.

'ACCESS DENIED,' said a computerised voice. ZIZZ! Sparks flew from the panel.

Stretch's hand shook violently and her purple hair stood on end. 'Ouch!' She yanked her arm away and blew on her fingers. 'It's all yours, buddy.'

Demon hesitated before placing his hand in the mould.

'ACCESS DENI – ' he whipped his arm away before the panel gave him the shock treatment, too.

Shrink clicked his boots to "walk mode", knelt down and felt along the bottom of the door. 'It's a perfect seal.'

'How about I melt a hole in it?' suggested Demon.

'Yeah, go on. Cool!' said Stretch.

Demon stared at the palm of his hand and thought about the heat bubbling away in his stomach, travelling up to his shoulders, then sending a burning sensation down his arms into his fingers. Any minute now, his hand would burst into flame.

A door banged shut somewhere nearby.

That will have to do. He placed his hand into the mould, hoping it was hot enough to melt the metal. 'ACCESS DENIED'. ZIZZ! His tail stuck up like a loo brush.

'I bash ze door down.' Wolfgang trotted to the end of the corridor. He turned and charged at the cupboard with his eyes narrowed, nose wrinkled and teeth gritted. Just before he hit the door he lowered his head, increased his speed and rammed into it. C-RANG!

The metal remained firm and free of scratches or dents. Wolfgang swivelled, staggered a few steps and keeled over.

Human Catapult

'What we need is more force,' said Stretch, as Demon helped Wolfgang to his feet. 'Find something heavy.'

Demon and Shrink discovered a hefty metal safe, the size of a microwave oven, in the "Safe Cracking" classroom. They struggled to carry it back to the passage.

'Guys, put it down at the other end of the hallway,' said Stretch. 'Then come back here, okay? I'm gonna need your help to turn me into a catapult.'

My dad wouldn't be doing the donkey work, thought Demon, frowning to himself. *He'd be in charge.*

Demon grasped Stretch around the waist and walked backwards, watching her arms grow longer and thinner.

They stretched easily, like elastic. Her
knuckles turned white from gripping the door
handles.

Demon felt his back touch the wall. 'Now what?' he asked.

'Put the safe on my stomach. And when I say "Now", let me go.'

With a lot of grunting, Shrink and Wolfgang heaved the safe onto Stretch. Tears welled up in her eyes with the bone-breaking weight of it.

'Now!' she shouted through gritted teeth.

Demon let go. TWWWAAAAANGG! Stretch pinged away from him at supersonic speed along the passageway. Two thirds of the way down it, he saw her jerk the safe into the air. Now it whistled towards the Secret Missions Store Cupboard under its own power. FFHEW!

Demon squeezed his eyes shut just before the moment of impact.

THOOOM!

When he opened his eyes there was a massive hole in the metal door. They'd done it! He slapped hands with Shrink and Wolfgang. 'Good work, Stretch,' he called.

'Thanks.' She turned her back on Demon, took a running leap, flipped over several times and finished tall in front of the broken door.

Demon joined her, stepping over a chunk of metal and clambering in through the hole. Inside, there were floor-to-ceiling shelves filled with gas masks, explosives, firearms, unbreakable lassoes, harpoons, maces, laser blasters and rows and rows of bottles. He picked up a small box, thinking it might be the sleep serum, but it was labelled "Flea Farm". *That might come in handy,* he thought and pocketed it.

'Here it is.' Shrink pulled a blue bottle off the shelf and showed him. On the label it read:

Sleep Serum

Directions: Add two drops to food to put someone to sleep for a week.

'We've got to put it in food,' said Demon.

'Thunderskull did tell us to bring some cake,' replied Stretch with a wicked grin.

*

At supper, Demon and his friends all chose cake for dessert. Then they sneaked the slices out of the dining hall and carried them to the bedroom which Demon, Shrink and Wolfgang shared. Demon turned the light off. Shrink pulled the blind down. Wolfgang blocked the keyhole with chewing gum and Stretch covered the portrait on the wall of Doctor Dynamite, one of the school governors.

'I think we're ready,' Demon whispered to his friends in the darkness. He sat on the floor with his back against the cold metal of the torpedo that was the base of his bed. The words "*Property of the USSR*" glowed on the grey bullet-shaped casing.

'I'll turn on my MTT,' said Shrink.

'What's that?' asked Demon.

CLICK! His friends' faces were lit in ghoulish green by a torch pen Shrink was shining at them. 'My Molecular Transparency Torch,' Shrink replied.

Demon noticed that, where the circle of green light rested on Wolfgang's cheek, he could see the bones under his skin.

'The MTT enables you to see through virtually anything,' said Shrink, shining it at the ceiling.

Demon saw the sole of a shoe and the back cover of a paperback book.

'That's what's on the floor upstairs,' said Shrink.

'Wow.' Demon felt something brush his shoulder. He looked behind him to see Stretch's arm extending across his mattress towards the items they'd gathered: a pair of rubber gloves, a bottle of sleep serum and a tray of cakes.

He grabbed the gloves and put them on. SNAP! Life would be wicked without Chill around for a few days.

'Sleep serum, please.' He held out his hand, like a surgeon in a hospital operating theatre.

Chill's Winter Wonderland

The four friends left the bedroom, carrying the spiked cakes. The passageway stank of rotten eggs from an industrial-strength stink bomb fight that had taken place earlier. Hard rock music boomed out from behind closed doors splattered with egg.

'What if they guess we're up to something?' asked Shrink. He held onto the edges of two plates of Death by Chocolate Cake – Wolfgang's and his own.

'Ve're in deep dung,' replied Wolfgang, as he trotted along beside him.

'Look on the bright side,' said Stretch, 'if we manage to send Chill *rock-a-bye-baby* the teachers will be seriously impressed. And, guys, it's not like you're on your own. I am helping you.'

You're helping us! Demon sniffed. He marched straight into a rope, which cordoned off a wall someone had walked through that morning. The rope came up to his chest, whereas Shrink's head was level with it.

Demon was about to ask him about this sudden size reduction when Stretch distracted him with a new idea.

'Even if they don't eat the you-know-what, we're gonna learn loads more about Chill and his uglies,' she said. '"*Keep your friends close and your enemies closer.*" That's what Doctor Super Evil said. It can be our plan B, right? He'll be so pleased when he finds out we've been listening in class.'

In no time at all, Demon and the others reached Chill's room. "Vicious" was scrawled in big, jagged green letters on the metal door. Demon felt an icy draught through his boots.

He knocked on the door. Stretch knocked louder.

Demon heard the crunch of feet, then a crack as the door came off its hinges. WHOOSH! A wheelbarrow's worth of powdery snow tumbled out into the passage. It covered Demon's feet, instantly making his toes cold.

'Oops!' Thunderskull propped the broken door against the wall. He wore mittens and a woolly jumper with a snowman motif over his school uniform. 'It's the slaves.' He stared at the plate in Demon's hand and smiled. 'And they've brought cakes fer the party!'

'Let them in,' said Chill. 'I'm just finishing.'

Thunderskull stepped to one side. Chill stood in the middle of the snow-covered bedroom, staring at the ceiling with white eyes. Wherever his gaze settled, glittering icicles appeared. KR-AAK-LL! They grew down a few metres, like swords unsheathing.

The four friends waded into the room and formed a tight huddle for protection at the bottom of Chill and his sidekicks' white beds. Demon shook with the cold. He could no longer feel his feet. Snow came up to his knees and poor Shrink's nose. Stretch rubbed her arms, but her teeth didn't chatter like wind-up joke teeth as his did.

Chill's eyes glinted, like the icicles he had created. He turned to the boy with big golden eyes, who waited by the door with Thunderskull. 'Dark Owl, I think we've found the firebug's weakness! What a shame, then, he's going to have to spend the evening in minus fifty degrees while he clears up my winter wonderland.' Chill's mouth curled into a nasty smile. 'And he hasn't even brought a spoon.'

Demon had forgotten about Chill telling them to bring spoons. Not that they would help to clear up all this snow. *We're not here to work anyway,* he thought.

Chill pushed past him to join his sidekicks at the door.

Demon tried to stop his teeth from chattering but couldn't. 'You a-a-asked f-f-for c-c-cake.' He thrust his plate at Chill and held his breath.

Chill sneered. 'No, I didn't, Thunderskull did, which for future reference counts for nothing. Do you really think I'd eat anything of yours?'

Demon felt as disappointed as if he'd had no presents on Halloween.

'Will you do the honours?' Chill said to Dark Owl.

'Mos' def', man.' Dark Owl stretched out his arms towards the cakes and flicked up his hands. The cakes flew off the plates – WHOOSH! – and hit Demon and his friends in their faces. SPLAT! Before Demon knew what was happening, icing and bits of sponge stuck to his skin. Chill and his sidekicks laughed.

Wolfgang made a rumbling growl as he wiped chocolate cream off his eyes. 'Zat's it!'

A small flame flickered from one of Demon's nostrils and then went out. 'L-l-let's gg-get th-th-them.' He lunged at Chill with the miniscule amount of energy he could muster.

CRACK! The sound came from above him. He looked up to see icicles breaking off and hurtling down on them.

Demon jumped to one side and narrowly missed being chopped in half by an icicle longer than him. THWAPP! It stuck into the snow like a garden cane. Stretch caught hold of Wolfgang by the scruff of his neck and yanked him out of the way of another. This one's end rammed into the snow, too. In a matter of seconds a ring of icicles surrounded Demon and the others like bars in a jail. They separated the friends from Chill and his gang and blocked off the door.

Too cold, thought Demon. With every second that passed he was finding it more and more difficult to concentrate on anything other than the pain in his bones. His body froze stiff.

Stretch reached through the bars with a long arm and punched Thunderskull on the forehead. WHAM! He just smiled at her. Tears flooded Stretch's eyes. 'Ouch! He's gotta mega hard nut.'

'We expect every single ice crystal to be gone by the time we come back,' said Chill from the doorway. He and his gang left, laughing.

Demon tried to yell out in fury, but his jaw had locked.

'Ve have to clear up ze snow,' said Wolfgang.

Demon moved his eyes (the only part of him he could move) from left to right to look for something they could use to help get them out. The only object not covered in snow was a corkboard with a map of the International Space centre pinned to it. One of the bullies had scrawled "School Project" on it. Even though his brain felt like an ice cube Demon realised they were up to something. *And we're going to find out what,* he thought.

'Vere's Shrink?' asked Wolfgang.

'I bet he's shrunk,' said Stretch.

Wolfgang sniffed the air then dived into the whiteness, sending a tidal wave of snow at Demon. He seemed to be under the snow for ages. Eventually, his head popped up. 'Can't find him anyvere.'

Super Simulator

Shrink had not been lost under the snow. He had slipped through the bars and run off to fetch buckets of boiling water to melt the ice. Even so, Demon spent the rest of the night defrosting in his bedroom and working on the extra homework Doctor Super Evil had set him. He felt sick with tiredness the next morning, which just happened to be his first session in the Super Simulator where his powers would be put to the test.

Approaching the room, he tried to strut like his super villain dad had done whenever meeting and defeating the general public. Hopefully the teacher wouldn't hear his two hearts thumping loudly in his chest.

The Super Simulator was larger than the other classrooms and shaped like a hexagon.

Demon could see a few First Years play fighting on the spectator gallery that ran around the top of the room. Just below the ceiling hung an electronic board with pupils' names and scores flashing in red. Stretch's name glowed at the top. She'd won the most points.

This is my chance to show them my super skills, Demon thought, remembering the head teacher's welcome speech.

He noticed doors on five of the room's walls and a window to an observation area on the sixth. Behind the glass sat Vera Vile, the teacher. She had pale green skin and wore dark glasses and a hat made of barbed wire.

'Another scrawny, wet-behind-the-ears, good-for-nothing First Year. How depressing.' Vera Vile sighed and picked up a clipboard.

'You are . . . Demon Kid.' She looked over the top of her glasses and inspected him with sharp eyes. 'You're not Demon *King's* son?'

'Yes, I am.' He puffed out his chest.

The teacher leaned closer to the window, looked him up and down and wrinkled her nose. 'You must take after your mother,' she said finally.

Laughter erupted from the gallery.

Demon's shoulders slumped. His mum wasn't famous like his dad. She made packed lunches for his father's fifty henchmen, drove the getaway vehicle and ferried Demon to his friends' houses in the family fighter jet. She was just an ordinary mum.

Vera Vile stared into the distance. 'I was with your father the night he boarded the Russian submarine and stole their torpedoes and nuclear warheads. What a night!' Her eyes re-focused on Demon. 'Your father would, no doubt, have been brilliant at this Simulator if St Viper's had been around in his day. Let's hope you don't let him down.'

Demon picked up his tail and nervously twisted it with hands swollen and purple from last night's misadventure.

Vera Vile flicked open a secret compartment in the chair arm to reveal a panel of buttons. 'The Super Simulator has been designed to help you develop your powers. Today, I will be testing how well you produce fireballs.' She touched a button. 'Let me introduce you to our R0K fighting robots.'

WHRRR! The doors opened to reveal five big and bulky robots. They were covered in lots of different sized boulders so that they looked like rock monsters. A red "0" flashed in the middle of their chests.

CLOMP. CLOMP. CLOMP! The robots entered the room and the ground shook. They surrounded Demon, leaving just a small space between them and him.

'You will score 200 points if you hit a robot on the chest with a fireball. And 50 points if it touches any other part of its body,' she said. 'You have twenty minutes to score as many points as you can. Now, do whatever it is you do to fire up.'

Demon took a few slow breaths in and out. He curled his hands into tight fists, squeezed his eyes shut and thought about lava bubbling, boiling and spitting in the pit of his stomach. He imagined scalding heat shooting up to his neck and down his –

R-R-R-MMBBLL! The ground trembled under Demon's feet.

I'm not ready! His hands felt cold and clammy, the complete opposite of what he needed. He tried to block the advancing robots out of his mind, but it was no good.

Demon opened his eyes. One of the robots tore a massive boulder off its chest, brought its arm back and flung the hefty lump of rock at him. Before Demon's brain clicked into gear the boulder hit him hard in the stomach - WAK! - punching the air out of his lungs. OOOF! His legs buckled and the force propelled him backwards through the air. WHOOM! He hit the reinforced glass window of the observation room - CRUNCH! - and slid down onto the floor. His body sang out in pain. The heavy boulder dropped onto his legs, squashing all the feeling out of them.

They're trying to kill me! he thought.

'Go on, finish him,' shouted a young villain on the balcony.

The R0K robots advanced. CLOMP. CLOMP. CLOMP! With gritted teeth Demon pushed at the boulder. He couldn't budge it.

Seeing Red

The robots halted mid-step.

'Stop being a numbskull!' Vera Vile's sharp voice crackled over the loud speaker. 'You must focus when you're making fire. Control your power - harness it. Black out all other thoughts.' She hammered on the glass. 'AND GET UP, YOU JIBBERING JELLYFISH!'

The robots clonked and clattered forward again. Demon pushed at the boulder with all his strength. This time it rolled off him. He scrambled to his feet and slowed his breathing. He clenched his hands into fists and thought about fierce heat.

'Feel the fireball forming,' said Vera Vile. 'Concentrate.'

Demon could feel something solid, round and hot form in his right hand. Slowly he uncurled his fingers. Small flames flickered in his left hand. In his right palm rested a swirling red and orange fireball, the size of a tennis ball. 'Yes!'

Out of the corner of his eye, he saw a boulder rolling along the floor towards him at breakneck speed. Demon curled his hand around the fireball to protect it and hurdled over the huge rock. It smashed against one of the doors. THOOM! He locked his eyes on his target and flung the fireball at the R0K robot. FWOOSH! The ball hit its body – POW! – and "200" points flashed on its chest.

Maximum points! Yahoo! Demon eyed the robot in front of him. *If I can do it once, I can do it again,* he thought.

He concentrated hard. Roasting heat raced down both his forearms into his clenched hands. Something firm and oven-hot pushed against his fingers, making them open. A quick glance down confirmed orangey-red fireballs inside both his fists. Demon spun and fired them off, one-two! POW! A "200" and a "50" flashed on two robots' chests.

Demon thrust his arms into the air. *I'm going to be number one on the leader board,* he thought. *The King - just like my dad.* He couldn't wait to phone home and tell his parents the good news.

Just then he felt a wallop above his ear. A boulder knocked him sideways. His head stung and eyes watered. R-R-RMMBBLL! The sound filled the room as several big, round stones thundered towards him. He managed to jump the first but the second knocked him off his feet. THOK! Then three slightly smaller boulders hit him in the face. His nose spurted blood.

Anger swelled inside Demon and took over him. He jumped to his feet, flicked out his claws and glared at the R0K robots. The whole room looked hazy and red.

'ARRGHHH!' He burst from head to toe into flames.

Demon could barely make out the outlines
of the robots behind the veil of raging fire, but
he charged forward. Using fists and feet he hit
out at anything and everything. WAK! BKOP!

PTHAP! His hearts raced and his skin streamed with sweat. He kept battling.

'Stop now,' said a faint voice. It seemed a long way off.

Demon kept punching.

'STOP NOW.'

Demon halted mid punch and looked around as his flames flickered out and the red haze cleared. The R0K robots were no longer in the room. *I've been fighting myself?*

On the gallery, the three young villains rolled around laughing.

Demon lowered his head.

'The game ended two minutes ago.' Vera Vile sucked in her cheeks and gazed at him over her glasses. 'How do you think that went?'

'Good to start with.' He bit his lip. 'But I don't know . . . I saw red.'

'You lost your head. That is what happened.' The teacher shook with rage. 'You must learn to control your power, you nitwit.'

She prodded a button and Demon's name appeared in last place on the electronic board. 'Now get out of my sight, son of *Mrs* King.'

Tears pricked Demon's eyes. His dad wouldn't have scored so badly in the Simulator or fallen into Chill's ice trap last night. *I'm a rubbish super villain*, he thought.

Building An Eraser Ray

On Friday morning Demon had Sinister Science, the subject he was most looking forward to studying. And with Chill away on a school trip he felt much happier. He sat with his friends at a workbench at the back of the class, wearing safety goggles and a protective apron. He couldn't wait to find out what crazy experiment they'd be doing.

'Mr Madness has asked me to remind you that you're supposed to be *proving* to the teachers that you are despicable. He's planning on sending school reports to your parents next Monday. So, you'd better get working on it,' said Professor Plutonium, the teacher who'd put Demon's flames out on the airship. He wore a white doctor's coat over canary-yellow and green tartan trousers.

Demon sighed. 'He's bound to write about my really low score in the Super Simulator.'

'Mine too,' replied Shrink. He rested his head in his hands.

'I'm expecting a fab report. My name *is* top of the leader board.' Stretch wiped a hand across her brow. 'Phew.'

Demon groaned.

'This term I am going to teach you about weapons and chemicals that make objects vanish into thin air or become invisible.' Professor Plutonium perched on a desk covered in bundles of dynamite, fuses and detonators. 'In this lesson we will build a common and highly effective vaporiser. Do any of you lab rats know what it might be?'

Demon looked at the box of atomiser chambers, metal gun grips, thermonuclear nuts, glass tubing and telescopes in front of him and then around at the other pupils. A few girls and boys had their hands in the air.

Stretch extended her arm so it was higher than everyone else's.

'The girl at the back.'

'An eraser ray,' answered Stretch.

'Correct.'

'Yes!' Demon said.

Professor Plutonium swept some bundles of dynamite to one end of his desk to make a clear space. He faced the class. 'I want you all to copy me. First, find a metal grip like this one.' He held up what looked like the handle of a gun, only bigger. 'And attach a trigger to it, like so.'

Demon followed the instructions. His tongue stuck out a little as he concentrated on putting the pieces together. Did the telescopic sight need to be attached to the top of the eraser ray before or after he inserted the atomiser chamber?

Shrink finished miles before everyone else. His vaporiser was the size and shape of a small fire extinguisher. It had three long metal barrels encased in a glass tube and a thick handle to hold onto. Demon looked closely at Shrink. He had come back from the Simulator the size of a toy soldier, but now he looked the biggest he'd ever seen him. *When he's confident he's big and when he's not he's small,* Demon thought.

'You need to screw the telescope on next,' Shrink said to Demon.

Someone's eraser ray went off near the front of the class. Demon saw the ray gun's glass tube glowing. Then out of its three barrels shot beams of luminous green light. ZZSSTT! They headed straight for the teacher! Professor Plutonium dived behind his desk for cover. A blinding flash followed.

His desk vanished.

Why didn't I think of vaporising him? Demon thought.

'First and final warning - there is instant dismissal for anyone who tries to vaporise a teacher or student,' said the Professor.

Professor Plutonium clambered to his feet and pointed a finger at the pupil holding the eraser ray.

Stretch tutted as she looked through the viewfinder. 'Not fair! We could have used it on Chill. That would have proved to Mr Madness that we're way more wicked than the other First Years and got rid of the bullies – permanently.'

'We'll just have to think of something else.' Demon's tail flicked the legs of his stool as he thought. 'Chill has to have a weakness. All villains do.'

'Or they want something really badly. Something we could get hold of first to spite them,' muttered Shrink.

'I haven't been able to find out any more about their school project.' Demon sighed. 'Space is a topic *ultra-ordinaries* would study. Not super villains. I don't get it.'

R-R-OARRR! The noise came from outside the classroom. Clouds of smoke billowed against the window. An alarm rang out.

'Either the volcano is erupting or some of the Senior Year are back from their school trip,' said Professor Plutonium. 'If it is the latter, the topic of your next lesson will be invisibility.' He grabbed two handfuls of glass test tubes from his desk and shoved them in the pockets of his doctor's coat. 'I'll collect some lava samples if it is an eruption,' he said to no one in particular. 'Okay, lab rats, form an orderly line and follow me.'

Girls and boys stampeded past Demon to the door.

'Take ze eraser ray,' Wolfgang whispered to Shrink and thrust it at him.

Demon turned to speak to Stretch, but her seat was already empty. He raced out of the classroom and along the passageway with Shrink and Wolfgang. Pupils poured out of all the doors, slowing them down.

In the airship launch area, teachers and pupils gathered on the walkway that ran around the inside of the volcano. Demon, Shrink and Wolfgang stuck close together.

'If the volcano is erupting we'll never get out in time!' shouted Shrink.

How To Steal A Rocket Ship

A blast of hot air blew back Demon's hair. Shrink held his hand up in front of his eyes to shield them from the extreme heat and Wolfgang gave a low growl.

A massive cone of orange flame lowered into the opening above them. R-R-ROARRR! The sound filled Demon's head. Then four white fins appeared followed by the long cylindrical, metal body of a rocket ship. The name "HERMES 01" was visible high up on the casing.

'Wow! I've never seen a spaceship in real life before,' Demon shouted. 'It's incredible.'

'Hmmm, do you think it has anything to do with Chill's school project?' asked Shrink.

'I don't know,' said Demon.

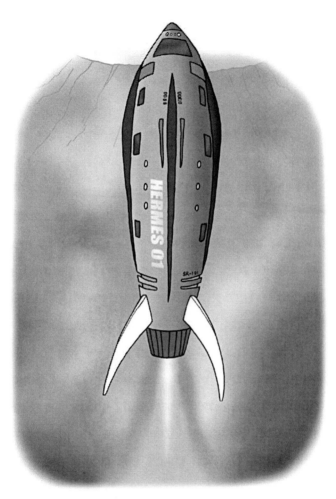

The cone of orange flame touched down on
the empty, circular platform. As it did so, a ring
of grey smoke and steam surrounded the
flames and billowed up around the rocket.

HISSSS! The spacecraft lowered into the steam.

Shrink tilted his head right back. 'Look up there!'

Demon saw a hatch opening. 'Are the astronauts coming out?'

'I zink so,' replied Wolfgang.

A silver ramp extended out of the hatch, bridging the gap between the spaceship and the wall of rock. The ramp grew longer until it reached a balcony on the upper level. CLUNK!

The crowd gasped. Demon had butterflies.

Four people clambered out of the hatch. They weren't in spacesuits, as Demon expected, but wore jeans and t-shirts like ultra-ordinaries. Although they were hundreds of metres up, Demon could still make out their faces.

His insides twisted.

Chill. He walked to the middle of the ramp with his head held high and shoulders back. His hands rested on his hips. Thunderskull,

Dark Owl and the girl with the eye mask posed beside him.

The crowd erupted into wild applause. 'Ch-ill. Ch-ill. Ch-ill.'

BOOM! Mr Madness danced the flamenco out of a cloud of green smoke, next to the base of the rocket ship.

He looked up at Chill and his sidekicks. 'I see your school trip was superbly successful.' He held his stomach and laughed, 'MWAHAHAHAHA.' The teacher gave the spacecraft a massive hug and a sloppy kiss. 'Come down and join us,' he said to Chill.

Why did it have to be them? Demon thought as he watched the bullies hold hands, step off the ramp and float like feathers down to the ground. Even Shrink seemed caught up in the moment. He was filming Chill on his cool watch.

'That's why they had a floor plan for the International Space Centre on their corkboard.

We could have stopped them,' Demon said to Wolfgang.

Mr Madness shook each of their hands. 'You have all earned a permanent place in the Syndicate of Supreme Evil. Dastardly done.'

'I've heard enough.' Demon trudged towards the nearest exit with his tail hanging limply behind him. Wolfgang followed him, both of them making slow progress because the launch area was so crowded.

'Do you want to know how we did it?' Chill asked the onlookers.

'YES!' the boys and girls all screamed.

He put a blue hand to his ear. 'I can't hear you.'

'YES!'

Chill laughed. 'Oh, all right, then.' He paused for a moment to keep the pupils in suspense. 'We hung around at the International Space Centre until it grew dark. On my command, Thunderskull head-banged the main gate down and got us into the hangar where the spaceship was kept.' Thunderskull flexed his muscles for the crowd. Chill continued, 'I disabled the security cameras by freezing them over.' He lifted his hands and they turned from blue to shimmering white. 'And Levitate, here, transported us up to the flight deck, right at the top of the spaceship.' The girl with the eye mask and messy hair held Chill's wrist and they floated a few feet off the ground and came back down again.

The crowd stomped their boots on the floor. It sounded like heavy thunder.

'Then, Dark Owl brought the spaceship back here.' Chill smiled at his accomplices. 'Stage one complete.'

'I thought there was only one stage,' said Mr Madness.

'What are you up to?' shouted several boys and girls together.

Chill swept a hand through his blue hair. 'I guess it won't hurt to tell you. In a few days, when no one can find the spaceship, a shed load of money will be stumped up for its safe return. My dastardly plan is to take the ship back to the International Space Centre, once the teachers have what they want, of course. And claim the reward.'

Mr Madness laughed. 'Now that is using your initiative! They seriously are super villains!' he said.

Demon froze mid-step in the doorway. 'I know how we can get our own back on Chill and give Mr Madness something bad to write about in our school reports,' he whispered to Wolfgang. 'Let's steal the spaceship from them. Right under their noses.'

'And claim ze reward!' added Wolfgang.

Demon stared at the spaceship and smiled.

'Mr Madness, I wanna be next to go up into space,' shouted Stretch, from the opposite side of the room to Demon.

That'll be me, Demon thought.

'No, choose me, me, me,' called out lots of boys and girls.

'My vile, venomous vipers, the spaceship hasn't been snatched to become play equipment for the school yard.' Mr Madness cackled at the thought. 'What we're after is contained within the cargo hold and is top secret.'

The Top Secret Solution

'We have it on abominable authority that inside the spaceship there is a state-of-the-art "invisibility sprayer".' Mr Madness rubbed his hands together with glee. 'It was due to be taken up into space to make certain USA satellites and spaceships undetectable for undercover operations. But we thought we could put it to uglier use.'

The head teacher pressed a button on the spaceship. CLUNK! HISSSSS! A hatch at ground level slowly opened. A small strip of light shone under the door. Demon balanced on tiptoes and craned his neck to get a better view over the other pupils' heads. He watched Mr Madness jiggling on the spot. Even Wolfgang stood upright for once.

'Imagine what our Syndicate of Supreme Evil could achieve if no one ever saw us coming?' said Mr Madness as he waited for the hatch to fully open.

'We could bulldoze Times Square?' suggested a girl with a lightning tattoo.

The teacher chuckled. 'Like it a lot!'

'Paint the Prime Minister in his sleep?' yelled Hammerhead from the front row.

'What fabulous fun!'

Mr Madness wiggled his eyebrows. 'It would save him the trouble of having to select a suit for work.'

'Take over the world!' shouted Demon.

Mr Madness slapped his thigh. 'Now you're talking!' he said in a loud voice, then dived in through the open hatch.

The cargo hold gleamed (except where Mr Madness' dirty hand and footprints touched its white surfaces) and was packed full of different-sized metal boxes. Mr Madness jumped up and down beside the biggest box. 'This must be it! I give thee the invisibility sprayer!' he shouted. 'Victory will be ours!'

Everyone, including Demon, held their breath.

The teacher flicked a metal catch on the box and the sides dropped to the floor. THUMP! Inside the container sat a dome-shaped lunar vehicle, the size of a small car. It had antenna dishes on the roof, docking lights, long landing legs and a ladder.

'Grrrr!' Mr Madness hunched his shoulders and clenched and unclenched his hands. Then he dragged a rectangular box into the doorway. 'Behold the invisibility sprayer,' he shouted again.

This one contained a satellite with long solar panels. 'No, that's not it!' he roared, tearing the lids right off three more boxes. R-R-RIPPP! 'Don't just stand still, help me!'

A mad scramble followed to get inside the cargo hold. Demon elbowed his way through the hatch and flung open two boxes at once. Chill might be the one who'd brought them the spaceship, but he would find the top secret sprayer.

'What does the invisibility sprayer look like?' asked a girl, as she rooted through the box next to Demon's. Scales protruded through the back of her jumpsuit.

'Leaked, top secret documents suggest it resembles a hand-held paint sprayer,' answered Professor Plutonium. 'It sprays objects in a special paint which alters their natural colour to match their backgrounds. It's an amazing camouflage device. We are led to believe that just one drop of paint is enough to cover the entire surface area of a room.'

Demon stroked the bubble helmet of a puffy white spacesuit he found inside a box and shivered with excitement. He couldn't wait to try it out in space! Soon the contents of every box, cupboard and locker lay strewn all over the cargo hold.

THUD! Demon turned to see Mr Madness banging his head against a locker.

'I don't understand. Scorpion Tail's third cousin has never imparted inaccurate information in the past!' he screamed at Professor Plutonium.

'Quite.' Professor Plutonium didn't try to stop Mr Madness hurting himself even though he was right next to him. He crossed his arms and tilted back his head. 'Of course, it is possible that the invisibility sprayer could be invisible itself.'

Mr Madness stopped giving himself a fractured skull and stared at Professor Plutonium. 'That would stop super villains from stealing it.'

'Precisely.'

The head teacher yanked on his horns to straighten them. 'Listen carefully, venomous vipers. I want you to start feeling around with your hands. Tell me, straight away, if you touch anything.'

'The sprayer will probably feel like a big water gun,' added Professor Plutonium.

Demon and the other pupils searched high and low all day, but by the evening the *invisible* invisibility sprayer had still not been found.

'We're still going to steal the spaceship,' Demon whispered to his friends as they made their way to supper.

'And if we find the invisibility sprayer, it'll be finders keepers,' added Stretch.

Snatching The Spaceship

A few hours later, in the dead of the night, Demon and his friends crept up to the top floor. Little cracks in the earthy walls glowed hot orange, illuminating their path.

Demon looked at Shrink flying along in his jet boots with weak blue flames spluttering out of the soles. The eraser ray that Shrink had made in "Sinister Science" stuck out of the rucksack on his back. *He must be nervous. He's getting smaller again,* Demon thought.

'I wish I had your super skill,' Demon said quickly.

'You do?' Shrink stopped getting any smaller.

'Yeah. You don't need invisibility paint to stop people seeing you coming, like the rest of us,' he said. 'You're really talented.'

'I guess so . . . Yes, I am.'

Shrink clicked the lever on his boots to "sport mode" and shot up into the air. WWHOOSHH! Vivid blue fire glowed beneath his shoes. As Demon watched Shrink growing back to his normal size he felt the two hearts hammering in his own chest. If his dad were with him, he wouldn't feel so nervous. *Dad could pull this off, no problem,* he thought.

He peered around a fountain of orange lava. At the end of the corridor, he saw Thunderskull on a balcony, overlooking the airship launch area. The big lump had his back to the spacecraft. He was lifting a bar with huge weights piled on either end of it, up and down. From the balcony, a narrow silver ramp ran all the way up to an open hatch at the top of the spaceship. As far as Demon could tell, the ship was empty.

'Right, does everyone remember what they need to do?' whispered Demon.

'Yes,' they all replied.

Demon smiled. 'Let's do it, then. Good luck, Shrink.'

Shrink reduced in size until he looked no bigger than a tiny insect flying in the air. Only the two miniature blue flames shooting from his boots gave him away. He saluted Demon and the others and then rocketed out from their hiding place.

Demon watched Shrink go.

He was flying flat out, just below the ceiling, towards Thunderskull on the balcony. His jet boots made a faint buzzing noise as they zoomed over the big bruiser's head.

Thunderskull looked up, let go of the weight and it crashed to the floor. KLANGGG! He reached up with a big hand and grabbed at Shrink who swerved to the side. 'I'LL GET YER!'

Demon turned to Wolfgang. 'GO!'

Wolfgang took a running leap over the fountain and charged straight up to Thunderskull. He growled, snarled and snapped at his knees.

'Easy now,' said Thunderskull with a wobble in his voice.

Demon searched for Shrink. He spotted two tiny blue flames near the spaceship's hatch. *Well done*, he thought.

Thunderskull was slowly bending down and reaching for the weight. 'Good dog-boy,' he said, keeping his eyes on Wolfgang.

'What's he doing?' whispered Stretch.

Demon watched Thunderskull yank one of the flat, circular weights off the bar.

'Fetch!' shouted Thunderskull, throwing the weight like a Frisbee down the corridor.

Wolfgang turned and started to chase after it, a huge grin on his face. The weight crashed through a wall - FAROOM! - and Wolfgang jumped through the hole after it.

'I'll handle this,' said Stretch. She ran out from her hiding position.

Demon could barely bring himself to watch. Stretch was better at fighting than him - not that he'd ever admit it - but Thunderskull would make mashed potato of her.

Stretch extended her arms until they reached Thunderskull. She wound them around his big body at super speed, pinning his legs together and trapping his arms by his sides.

His face turned purple and he jerked about as he tried to break free.

'GO!' said Stretch, through gritted teeth.

Demon sprinted onto the balcony and up the bouncy, silver ramp. He glanced down at the bottom of the chamber far below and raised his tail to help him balance as he hurried across.

At the other end, Shrink scurried around inside the hatch, growing bigger.

'HAH!' shouted Thunderskull.

Demon glanced back over his shoulder. The big brute had broken free of Stretch's extra long arms and was tying them together in a knot.

'This is fun,' said Thunderskull as he twisted Stretch's limbs.

'Hey, get off me you big baboon,' she replied.

Forgetting the danger, Demon raced back across the ramp. His face grew hot. Smoke poured out of his ears and nostrils.

'Let her go,' he shouted as he ran.

We Have Lift Off!

Thunderskull laughed and twisted Stretch's arm. She screamed. Demon's head pounded. Flames flickered out of his skin. But then he remembered Vera Vile's words: "You must focus when you're making fire. Control your power – harness it."

Demon concentrated hard and channelled the intense heat from his stomach up to his neck and into his mouth. He blew out a great gust of red and orange flames - FFWOOSH! - roasting Thunderskull's eyebrows off. The big bruiser let go of Stretch to feel where they had been and moaned. The smell of singed hair filled the air.

Demon flicked his tail towards Stretch. 'Grab it!' he shouted.

She grasped hold of Demon's tail as best she could with her arms still tied together.

Demon bent down and grabbed the edge of the ramp to brace himself. 'Jump,' he said and she leapt off the balcony and swung up onto the ramp using his tail as a rope. He winced with pain. Tears filled his eyes.

'Thanks,' breathed Stretch, as she clung onto the narrow ramp next to Demon.

He rubbed the top of his tail. 'It's half a metre longer!'

The ramp bounced as Wolfgang landed next to them. BOINGG! He had the weight firmly clamped in his teeth. Demon raced towards the hatch, pulling Stretch along with him. Wolfgang charged behind them.

'You're frozen food,' Chill shouted from the balcony.

Demon felt like his hearts had jumped into his mouth. The ramp bounced up and down. He knew Chill and Thunderskull were on their heels.

'Shrink! Shut the hatch as soon as we're inside!' yelled Demon.

The friends leapt through and Shrink yanked the hatch down. CLUNK.

THUD! The two pursuers rammed the steel door on the other side, making the metal ripple. It wouldn't hold for long.

Demon untied Stretch's arms, then jumped into a seat and wriggled into the restraint harness. He lay on his back with his legs in the air. A silver control panel full of computer screens, dials, gauges, clocks, buttons and switches was in front, overhead and to the sides of him. Labels such as "Tachometer", "Cabin Pressure" and "Engine Temperature" meant nothing to Demon.

'Who's down to fly the spaceship?' he asked, keeping one eye on the hatch.

His friends shook their heads vigorously and looked blank.

'I'll do it,' said Stretch, jumping into the seat next to Demon. She stared blankly at the hundreds of buttons on the control panel.

'Actually guys, Shrink should. He's good with gadgets.'

KERRRUNCH! The metal door buckled inwards.

'There's got to be an autopilot.' Shrink flicked switches and pushed buttons.

KRAKK! 'I'm going to deep freeze the lot of you!' screamed Chill from the other side.

Demon started thumping random buttons, as did Stretch and Wolfgang. He hit "Engage" and the next second several dials spun from 0 - 30,000 on their gauges. Lights flashed. Alarms buzzed. The spaceship vibrated.

'That's not the autopilot, Demon!' shouted Shrink.

'We are GO for launch,' said a computerised voice. '10, 9, 8, 7, 6, 5, 4, 3, 2, 1. We have lift off!'

Wolfgang whined. His ears lay flat against his head.

The spaceship rocketed out of the volcano like a bullet blasting from a gun.

Demon and his friends were pushed back hard in their seats. The enormous craft vibrated from side to side, making Demon's head shake and teeth rattle. R-R-ROARRRRR!

The sound of the engines hurt his ears. When he didn't have his eyes squeezed tightly shut, he glimpsed hazy colours - blue and white - from the window directly in front of him.

Demon wondered how far into outer space they would fly with no one in control of the rocket ship: to galaxies millions of light years away? *I'll never be able to sit still that long*, he thought. Then he realised he'd be as dead as a dinosaur by the time he got there.

'Bye, Mum. Bye, Dad,' muttered Shrink.

Demon thought of his own dad. He always had faith that he would make it as a super villain. *If Dad believes in me, I should too*, he told himself.

Demon opened his eyes and studied the control panel with its fluctuating dials, coloured bar charts and speed counter. To the side of his chair he spotted a joystick. *My game console at home has one of those!*

He grabbed the joystick's round handle. 'Hold on tight!'

More Trouble

Demon and his friends slammed against their straps. The sky tilted. Demon's stomach rolled horribly. For a split second, he sat in a comfortable upright position, but then turned upside down.

'This is so cool!' shouted Stretch.

'Make it stop!' shrieked Shrink. His face had turned the colour of mushy peas.

With a sweaty hand, Demon pulled back a fraction to roll the ship the right way up. They flashed through thick cloud, over the sea. The roaring eased and the shaking turned into a vibration. Demon loosened his grip on the joystick. His fingers felt stiff from holding it so tightly. *I can't believe I'm flying a spaceship!* he thought. *Not my dad - me!*

'I'm gonna have a feel around for the invisibility sprayer,' said Stretch. 'Wolfie, are you coming?' She jumped out of her seat and disappeared through a hatch into the next compartment, at the back of the flight deck. Wolfgang scratched out a few fleas and trotted after her.

'I'll fly around the world until you find it,' said Demon, with a huge grin.

'Shall I carry on looking for the autopilot command?' asked Shrink. 'I'm not sure which way we should head for the International Space Centre.'

'Good idea,' replied Demon. 'The sooner we get the spaceship there, the sooner we get the reward money.'

Shrink tapped various buttons on the control panel. Drop-down lists appeared and disappeared. Lights flashed. 'I've just found a radio,' he said. 'I'll see if I can tune into the news.'

Demon caught snatches of pop music and then heard a very serious-sounding voice. 'This morning we bring you the latest on the missing spaceship. We also have new information on the submarine that vanished without trace six months ago. And we will be talking to Captain Cool about whether it really is cool to be saving the world 24/7.' The newsreader paused. 'Our top story – thousands of soldiers, policemen, secret agents and super heroes have been deployed to find the Hermes 01 –'

Demon winced. *That's all we need,* he thought. He pulled back on the joystick to take them higher.

'We have breaking news just in,' continued the reporter. 'The International Space Centre is going to pay a million dollars to whoever finds the spaceship.'

'Yahoo!' Demon looked over his shoulder at the open hatch. 'Stretch, Wolfgang, they've stumped up the reward!'

He heard a cheer and a bark.

'Oh, troll's toenails!' said Shrink, pointing.

Demon turned and followed Shrink's finger, out of the window. A fuzzy ball of blinding light zoomed towards them. SHHOOOM! It grew bigger by the second. Demon had a bad feeling about it.

'Maybe it's a comet,' he said. Then he heard the distant sound of a song: *I'm texting a hero*. Suddenly he saw the face of Mr Awesome, the chiselled-jaw good guy.

He flew along with his gold cloak flapping out behind him. A small movie camera sat on top of one of his bullet-deflecting wristbands.

Demon jerked the joystick hard left to turn the spaceship around.

BANG! Demon jolted forward against his straps and saw Mr Awesome staring in through the window. His theme tune blared into the rocket ship.

'They've brought in a super hero!' Demon shouted, hoping Stretch and Wolfgang would hear him in the next compartment. 'Get back here. Quick.'

Mr Awesome pointed the lens of his movie camera in through the window.

Demon stabbed the rocket-booster button with an outstretched claw. ROARRR! The sound drowned out Mr Awesome's theme tune, but then the engines started to screech. He glanced out of a side window at a cloud that looked like a one-eyed alien. 'We're not moving! He must be holding us here!'

Stretch and Wolfgang hurried through the hatch and jumped back into their seats. 'No way! Mr Awesome's come for a fight. Cool!' said Stretch.

Demon kept pushing the same button over and over again.

The super hero ran his fingers through his golden locks and rubbed his front teeth to make them sparkle. Then he turned the camera towards himself and spoke into a small microphone pinned to his jumpsuit. 'I, Mr Awesome – number one super hero in the solar system, world record holder for press-ups on one finger with a monster truck strapped to my back – ask whether you are friend or foe?'

Mr Awesome's Weakness

Mr Awesome gave the camera a winning smile and swivelled the lens to face Demon and the others.

'We've got to get away from him!' said Demon. He jerked the joystick forwards, sideways, backwards and forwards again, rolling himself and his friends upside down and inside out – or at least, that's how it felt.

'I don't feel very well,' complained Shrink.

Demon glared out of the window at Mr Awesome who was flattening his hair for the next camera shot.

'You guys, I've got an idea,' said Stretch. 'When I say, "Go", take us straight up, Demon.'

'What are you planning?' he asked.

Stretch rolled her eyes. 'Just trust me, okay?' She reached out with a long arm and rapped on the window. 'HEY MISTER - YOU'VE GOT MONSTER ZITS ALL OVER YOUR FACE.' She pointed at Mr Awesome and then at her own nose, cheeks and chin.

Mr Awesome shook his head and put an ear to the glass.

'YOU HAVE ZITS. HUGE, PUS-FILLED ONES. ON YOUR FACE!'

The super hero jerked away from the glass with wide-open eyes. He pressed a button on the top of the movie camera and felt his skin with both hands.

'GO!' she shouted.

Demon pulled the joystick back hard. They shot upwards. The sky slanted and their seats tilted until they were lying down with their feet in the air. The booster rockets roared, the compartment shook and they shot through clouds with Mr Awesome hot on the spaceship's tail fins. WHOOSH! The higher they flew, the darker it became and the smaller the super hero looked.

Demon stared out of the side window. There was no sign of Mr Awesome's dazzling, pearly whites in the blackness. 'I think we've lost him,' he said.

'Or he's gone home to squeeze his zits,' suggested Stretch with a grin.

Thousands of miles below, Planet Earth looked like the model globe in Demon's old junior school, except there were no place names on it, which was really unhelpful.

'Any luck with finding the autopilot command?' Demon asked Shrink.

His friend pressed a few buttons on the control panel in quick succession. 'I think this could be it.'

"Outside Temperature - 270 degrees C."

Shrink pushed his glasses up his nose and carried on tip tapping. 'Got it!' he said, eventually.

Demon followed Shrink's gaze and looked at a drop-down list on the screen.

Autopilot Destinations:

Space Satellite

Orbit

All Nations Space Station

International Space Centre

The Moon

'Brilliant! Once we've found the invisibility sprayer we can go straight to the International Space Centre,' said Shrink.

Demon felt a buzz of electricity in his tail as he read the last location on the list. 'It would be a shame to come all this way and not visit the moon,' he said.

'Zat's bad idea,' said Wolfgang. Demon noticed his friend's muscles had started to twitch under his skin.

Shrink turned to face Demon. 'We're supposed to be looking for the invisibility sprayer, not sight-seeing.'

'But we can look for it on the way there.' Demon grasped his friend's arm with excitement. 'We'd get to wear spacesuits and walk on the moon's surface and make a speech to the world. This is one small step for humans, one big step for villain-kind,' he said in his deepest voice.

'Cool! None of the other First Years will be able to beat that.' Stretch grinned.

'I guess it is a once-in-a-lifetime chance,' added Shrink.

'Okay! What are we waiting for. Let's go!' Stretch extended her arm and touched "The Moon".

Demon felt the spaceship tilt to the right.

'Turn ze ship around,' growled Wolfgang.

'Come on, Wolfgang. It will be fun,' said Demon.

'Volfgang vant to go back.' He reached out a hairy hand and hit "International Space Centre" on the screen to change their destination. THUMP!

Demon hit "The Moon". 'We can't take the spaceship back yet. We haven't found the invisibility sprayer. Don't you want to take over the world?'

'GRRRRRR!' Wolfgang snarled at him and whacked "International Space Centre" again, but the screen had frozen on Demon's last command.

'You've broken the computer!' Shrink held his head in his hands. 'How are we going to get home now?'

Moon Magic

Demon pushed the joystick this way and that but the spaceship stayed on the same course. He stared out of the window, nibbling on a claw. The blackness seemed to go on for ever.

Just then, a dozen or so bone-shaped biscuits floated past Demon's nose and up into the air. Wolfgang slipped out of his restraint harness and rose up after them. More dog biscuits, chewed rulers and well-slobbered pens came out of the tool belt around his waist.

'Wait for me!' said Demon.

'And me!' the others cried.

Demon clicked open his harness and rose up to join Wolfgang. 'This is great!' he shouted and rolled head over heels. 'I feel as light as a balloon.'

'Everything's weightless in outer space,' explained Shrink, pushing his escaping glasses back down. He glided off his chair with his arms stretched out in front of him. 'Look at me, I'm the Flying Phantom.'

Demon glanced at Stretch opening a locker below the control panel. Out of the cabinet floated little drink cartons with straws sticking out of them.

Stretch grabbed a carton, drifted up to join the others and read the label. 'Anyone for liquidised sausage, mash and tomato ketchup?' she asked.

'Me!' said Demon.

Wolfgang growled at him. 'MINE!'

Stretch squeezed the carton with both hands and blobs of brown liquid squirted up out of the hole. Wolfgang went after the puddles of food floating in the air like he hadn't eaten for weeks.

'I can see the moon,' called Shrink from the window.

Demon stared out of the spaceship at a grey-white orb, illuminated by the sun. It had lots of pits and craters from being bombarded by meteors over millions of years.

'Wow!' he gasped. 'It's amazing.'

HOWWWWWLL! Without any warning Wolfgang let out a spine-chilling noise. Demon watched in horror as his friend flung himself around.

'If he's doing what I think he's doing, we're in BIG trouble,' he yelled.

Black fur had sprouted all over Wolfgang's face and neck, his nose had elongated and a rubbery tip was appearing on its end. His fingers shortened into paws and his nails lengthened to razor-sharp claws. He thrashed around and kicked out with his arms and legs.

'Werewolf alert!' shouted Shrink.

Wolfgang slobbered, snarled and snapped at his tiny friend. GRRR!

Demon and Shrink pushed off the wall to get away from Wolfgang, but the flight deck was so small they couldn't find anywhere to hide.

Stretch extended her arms and yanked down the shutters to block out the moon. That didn't work. Wolfgang bared his newly grown fangs.

Demon snatched one of the cartons and squeezed the fluid into the air. 'Wolfgang, rr-roast dinner,' he stammered.

The werewolf stopped thrashing around and slurped up the floating fluid noisily.

Demon put his pocket-sized friend down on the control panel. 'You've got to turn the spaceship around.'

'But the screen's frozen.' Shrink shook his head at the computer display.

'I know you can do it,' said Demon.

With the carton empty, Wolfgang went back to gnashing his teeth and swiping at Demon with his claws.

Demon grabbed another carton of food with trembling hands. 'Wolfgang, stir fry?'

The werewolf lunged at him before he had a chance to squeeze out the contents of the

115

carton. But mid-leap, he stopped as though he'd been zapped with a freeze gun. KLONK! His head snapped back and he flew backwards, very slowly, into the wall. He hung limp in the air. A red lump bulged on his forehead.

'What was that?' said Demon, as Wolfgang's unconscious form turned back into a boy.

'C'mon, he musta hit the invisibility sprayer!' Stretch pushed off the wall. 'I'm gonna find it before you!'

'No you're not!' Demon felt all around the area where Wolfgang had bumped into the invisible, invisibility sprayer. Nothing. If Miss Competitive found it before him he'd never hear the end of it.

After a good five minutes of searching, Demon's elbow knocked against something hard in mid-air. He swivelled and touched the spot where his elbow had been. His hearts leapt. It had to be the sprayer!

The Unwelcome Party

Demon's fingers ran over a long, balloon-shaped nozzle and down a grip with deep grooves. The invisibility sprayer felt like a big water gun, just as Professor Plutonium said it would. He clasped the handle.

'I'VE FOUND IT,' he shouted. As he spoke, the special spy pen he'd given Wolfgang to chew bobbed in front of his face.

I wonder, he thought.

Stretch glided past Wolfgang, who was snoring in his sleep.

'Hey, give me the sprayer,' Stretch said to Demon.

'Just one minute.' Demon rubbed the end of the spy pen over the sprayer. A patch of yellow plastic appeared. Demon smiled at Stretch and she smiled back.

'Pleeeease let me have it.' She looked at Demon with big puppy dog eyes. 'Or I'll bust your nose.'

'You'd better come over here,' said Shrink in an anxious voice, still staring at the frozen computer screen.

Demon pushed hard off the wall and joined Shrink in front of the control panel.

SYSTEM OVERRIDE INITIATED BY MISSION CONTROL.

DESTINATION: INTERNATIONAL SPACE CENTRE

'Brilliant. The Space Centre are bringing us back in.' Demon held onto the back of his seat to stop himself from floating up to the ceiling.

'Fab!' added Stretch. 'We can sit back and relax now we've found the invisibility sprayer.'

'Are you crazy?' said Shrink. 'They're going to think we're the ones who've stolen the spaceship. Not Chill. Mr Awesome must have told them about us flying

118

away from him. That's why they're overriding the system. We're in serious trouble.'

'Trouble.' Demon grinned. 'My favourite word.'

*

By the time they landed, Wolfgang had eaten all the emergency food provisions, having woken up starving hungry. Demon nibbled his claws down to the fleshy, pink skin with nervous excitement.

CLUNK. JUDDER. HISS! A voice from the other side of the hatch boomed: 'Come out with your hands up.'

Demon jumped out of his seat and waited in front of the buckled door with the others. 'Shrink, have you got that special torch with you?' he asked.

'Yes.' Shrink unzipped the front pocket of his rucksack, pulled out his MTT and shone it at the hatch. A circle of green light appeared on the creased metal. Inside the circle, Demon saw through it to a short tunnel with a wide doorway at the end. Policemen with guns crowded around outside.

'They've sent a welcome party,' said Demon.

'Guys, there are only six cops. We can easily vaporise them with the eraser ray,' said Stretch.

'You're mad.' Shrink pulled his bulging rucksack closer to him. 'They'll hunt us to the ends of the earth if we start vaporising policemen.'

'And your problem with that is?' Stretch lifted her hands, palms facing upwards.

'Why don't we try lying to the policemen first?' suggested Demon. 'We'll say we're innocent . . . and that we didn't mean to fly away from Mr Awesome. And that we've come to claim the reward.'

'It is a lotta dough,' replied Stretch. 'I'll give it a go.'

'All right.' Shrink shuffled on the spot.

'But I can nip zeir ankles,' said Wolfgang. He had great rips in his jumpsuit and scratches all over his face.

'Only if things don't go to plan,' replied Demon. 'On the count of three we'll go out. Agreed?'

His friends nodded.

Demon grabbed hold of the hatch lever, as did the others. 'One. Two. Three.'

They pulled upwards, opened the hatch and the compartment filled with a cool breeze. With Stretch by his side, Demon swaggered through the short tunnel towards the policemen. Wolfgang pushed in between them and Shrink walked at the rear. The policemen aimed at their chests.

Demon's brain froze. 'We come in peace,' was all he could think to say as they reached the six gunmen in the doorway.

'You're making us sound like aliens,' hissed Stretch.

Demon glanced at Stretch and noticed her eyelashes lengthen.

She fluttered them at the policemen. 'Hi. I'm a girl scout and my friends are boy scouts and we're doing our neighbourly duty bringing the spaceship back to you.'

'Put your hands in the air.'

Demon jumped. 'You've made a mistake. We really didn't steal the rocket ship.'

'I told you they'd say that,' came a familiar ice-cold voice.

Guilty Until Proven Innocent

The cluster of policemen parted to let Chill and his sidekicks through. Demon clenched his reddening fists. He now saw that the doorway led to a large room full of policemen and soldiers looking down the barrels of rifles. There were cameramen, too. Some of them took cover behind cabinets containing stuffed chimps in spacesuits and old moon-landing vehicles.

Demon's insides churned. 'I hadn't expected quite so many people,' he said. A deluge of cameras flashed. The bright light hurt his eyes. He shielded his face with his claws.

'I bet you're not feeling so clever now are you, firebug?' Chill stopped on the other side of the doorway. 'For a crime like this, they'll lock you up in Doom Doors jail for the rest of your life.'

An electric current of fear shot down Demon's tail. His grandad still screamed whenever he heard the jangle of keys and he'd been out of Doom Doors for thirty years.

Chill turned to speak to a military man with medals pinned to his uniform. 'Now about that reward. A million dollars, wasn't it?'

'I've got it right here,' said the general. He lifted up a leather briefcase and smiled for the cameras.

'Don't give it to him!' yelled Demon. 'He's the thief!'

General Honeychurch smiled through gritted teeth. 'Take them away,' he ordered.

'Now ve fight?' asked Wolfgang.

'There are too many of them. We won't win,' replied Demon.

A group of policemen frogmarched Demon and his friends through the room. Chill made an "L" for loser sign with his thumb and finger.

Demon whacked a glass cabinet with his tail in anger. WHOP! 'If only we'd gone along with Mr Awesome rather than trying to shake him off, the police might have believed us,' he said to his friends.

'We got carried away,' added Stretch.

'Wait a minute! So did they!' Shrink stopped walking. 'Chill got carried away, too!' he said, sounding strong. 'All villains have a weakness. And Chill's is that he likes to boast.'

Demon, Stretch and Wolfgang looked puzzled. 'Get a move on,' said one of the policemen.

'Please, listen,' said Shrink. 'Remember Chill telling everyone how they stole the spaceship? I filmed him saying it!' Shrink pressed a button on the side of his multifunctional watch. Then he turned his arm around, so that the policeman could see the pictures on the face.

'Well I never!' The policeman radioed a colleague at the other end of the room. No reply came.

Demon could see General Honeychurch handing Chill the briefcase of money!

'They are the thieves,' Demon shouted, pointing a finger at the big kids. 'And we'll prove it to you!'

A beam of light shot out of Shrink's watch face and shone on to a bare wall in the room. A cinema-screen-sized picture came into focus. It showed Chill and his sidekicks standing in front of the rocket ship back at St Viper's. 'Do you want to know how we did it?' Chill said, loud and clear. Demon couldn't believe how much noise something so small could make.

The room fell silent. The cameramen swung their lenses towards Chill, Thunderskull, Dark Owl and Levitate. Now flashes went off in *their* faces.

'Get that watch!' Chill snapped at his henchmen.

Thunderskull charged towards them, like a gorilla in a game of rugby, flattening soldiers and policemen in the process. Wolfgang ran out to meet him. 'GRRRR! You vant trouble? I give you trouble.'

Dark Owl stared at Shrink, opened out his hand and made a beckoning motion with his fingers. The watch pulled away from Shrink's wrist, without anyone touching it.

Demon slapped a hand over it, as did Shrink. But the strap ripped in half - SNAP! - and the watch shot through their fingers. It flew through the air towards the thug at incredible speed. WHOOSH!

'Oh no you don't!' Stretch reached out with a long arm and grabbed it, but the watch continued moving towards Dark Owl. Her arm grew longer and longer as she tried to keep hold. Demon grabbed her outstretched arm and started gathering it in like a piece of rope, but her arm kept lengthening.

'I'll distract him,' said Shrink, beginning to reduce his size. He clicked a switch on his boots to "fly mode" and zoomed off.

Demon didn't have a chance to watch Shrink in action. Chill and Levitate were heading for him and Stretch. The briefcase full of money swung in Chill's bony hand. 'Your expiry date has passed,' he said.

'The *real* thieves have the money,' cried General Honeychurch. 'Arrest them.'

Policemen and soldiers tried to block their path. Chill blew cold air at them - TCCHOO! - and they instantly froze stiff. No one was coming to Demon's rescue. He had to fight his own battle.

I stole the spaceship from under your nose, thought Demon. *I flew it all by myself. And I've been trapped in a small space with a hungry werewolf.* He glared back at Chill. *I'm not scared of you.*

First Years Fight Back

Demon breathed in and out, clenched his hands and concentrated hard, just as Vera Vile had told him. When he uncurled his fists, a scorching fireball rested in both palms. He brought his arms up behind his head, gritted his teeth and swung his arms forward, sending the two fireballs flying towards Chill. FWOOSH! They sizzled and spat as they flew through the air. But they rapidly burnt up their energy and got smaller by the second. The fireballs fizzled out before they got anywhere near to Chill and Levitate.

'This takes me back to my First Year. Of course, unlike you, I came out top of the class.' Chill curled and uncurled his hand to reveal a cannonball of ice.

He gripped it in his blue fingers, took aim and sent it curving towards Demon. POW!

The ice ball hit Demon's left side - THOK! - knocking him backwards. His shoulder throbbed with pain. It felt like being with the R0K robots again. Demon's face grew hotter and the room turned red. *I mustn't lose control,* he thought.

Above his head, he heard a ping as Stretch's arm shortened to its normal size. He glimpsed Shrink's watch in her hand.

Demon scrambled to his feet and turned his attention back to Chill.

'Let me show you what we're learning in *my* year.' Chill stretched out an arm and a streak of frost blasted from his palm - K-K-R-AKKLL! - and grew into a gigantic wall of ice. Its crest scratched the ceiling as it rolled towards Demon like a tidal wave. A soldier stepped in front of him and started firing bullets at the icy wall - BANG! BANG! BANG! - but shards of ice shot back at him like miniature missiles. WHOOM! The wall hit the soldier head on and tumbled him over and over.

Chill's super skills are much better than mine. There has to be another way to beat him, Demon thought.

His tail flicked against something on the floor. He glanced down at Shrink's rucksack. *The eraser ray!* he thought and yanked it out of the bag.

Demon aimed the ray gun at the giant ice wall and pulled the trigger. The handle grew warm, the glass tubing glowed and the weapon juddered as its deadly energy built up inside. Three beams of luminous green light shot out of its barrels. ZZSSTT! With a blinding flash the wall vanished.

Now Demon looked at Chill through the telescopic sight.

Demon swallowed. It was one thing to imagine pulling the trigger of an eraser ray on someone. It was another to do it for real.

'What are you waiting for? Cold feet?' Chill laughed. 'You haven't got the guts to be a super villain. You're not your father.'

No, I'm not, thought Demon. *I'm me.*

CLANG! Demon took his eyes off Chill for half a second and glanced up to see Levitate floating in the air, holding her head. It looked like Stretch had knocked her against the shell of a rocket suspended from the ceiling by a thick chain. As Demon's eyes darted back, he spotted a space capsule hanging above Chill's head.

Perfect.

'Well, if you can't finish this, I will,' said Chill.

Demon steadied his grip and aimed straight into Chill's eyes. 'Oh yeah?' he said and squeezed the trigger.

Million Dollar Madness

Chill's face turned from sneer to horror as he realised he was about to be vaporised. But at the last second Demon swung the barrels upwards. The lurid green beams shot out of the gun and struck the chain holding the old space capsule over Chill's head. ZZSSTT! The chain vanished with a blinding flash.

Chill stood rooted to the spot with terror. The heavy metal object, about the size of a small car, fell towards him. His skin turned white and his hair crusted with snow. Stretch whipped out a long arm at super speed and snatched the briefcase out of Chill's hand just before the empty shell crashed down on top of him. KLANGGG!

Demon noticed that everyone in the room had stopped fighting. The cameramen directed their lenses towards the crumpled heap of wreckage where the space capsule had landed on Chill. Demon quickly stuffed the eraser ray into Shrink's rucksack before the cameramen turned to him. As the cloud of dust and snowflakes settled, he saw a huge chunk of ice with smashed up pieces of metal tangled around it. Inside the ice block stood Chill, frozen into a frightened pose, flinching away from the falling capsule.

'Is he dead?' asked Shrink, buzzing over to Demon and Stretch.

'Nah,' replied Stretch. 'I can see his chest moving. But he's gonna take a while to chill out.' She grinned.

'Don't worry, we'll see that he's dealt with when he emerges,' said the general, marching up behind them. 'And we'll take good care of his accomplices too.'

Demon looked around to see Chill's henchmen being led away in handcuffs.

'You ain't heard da last of me,' shouted Dark Owl, shaking a fist.

Levitate fought every step of the way to the door, like a cat being given a bath and

Thunderskull trudged along, sniffing. His backside poked through a hole in his trousers.

'Zat vas fun,' said Wolfgang, joining Demon and the others. He had a square of material in his mouth.

They all smiled and slapped hands. Everyone in the room applauded.

General Honeychurch patted Demon on the back. 'You children well and truly deserve the million dollar reward.' He frowned at Demon's jumpsuit. 'Tell me, what school do you go to?'

BOOM! A cloud of green smoke appeared. Mr Madness, the head teacher, strolled out of the mist, wearing a top hat and a woman's flowery apron.

'He must have found those clothes in the store cupboard!' whispered Shrink.

Demon tried not to laugh.

'There you are, First Years. We've been worried about your well-being.' Mr Madness pulled them close to him, half strangling

Demon. 'Where's the invisibility sprayer?' he spat.

'We don't know, sir,' said Demon, but Shrink glanced at the bulging rucksack.

Mr Madness snatched it off him. Then he pulled a mannequin's plastic hand out of his apron pocket and offered it to General Honeychurch to shake. But he didn't take his shiny eyes off the briefcase, which Stretch held. 'I am Mr Madness, head teacher of St Vi - Violet's School for . . . *circus performers*.'

The General smiled and nodded. 'That's why they're in jumpsuits and can produce fireballs and make their arms really long! I thought they might be young super heroes!'

Mr Madness laughed. 'Super heroes! Not in a million years!'

KNOCK. KNOCK. KNOCK! Demon saw Mr Awesome banging on one of the room's windows. 'Have I missed anything?' he shouted.

'Our departure is overdue,' Mr Madness said to General Honeychurch. Then he hurried Demon and the others to a quiet spot. 'Give me the briefcase,' he ordered Stretch.

She hesitated. 'You'll give it back, yeah?'

'Of course.' Mr Madness took the briefcase off her. 'I believe our business here is over.'

'What about Chill and his gang?' asked Shrink.

A puddle had formed where the ice block had started to melt. Demon could see Chill inside it trying to make a fist.

'The best baddies won.' Mr Madness hugged both the bag and briefcase and smiled round at Demon and his friends.

'But won't they be sent to Doom Doors jail?' asked Demon.

'Yes.' Mr Madness shrugged. 'It's an occupational hazard. Most super villains spend a spell in the slammer at some stage. Luckily the school has a very good "Long Distance Learning" programme - all communicated in code, of course.' He glanced in the direction of the window. 'Now grab my belt and for badness' sake don't let go unless you want to become a shark snack.'

Demon and his friends caught hold of the flimsy belt with both hands. BOOM! A cloud of thick green, cheesy-feet-smelling smoke engulfed them. Wind whipped their faces and howled in their ears. Demon's legs floated out behind him and his fingers ached from grasping the belt so tightly. He wasn't sure where he was or if he could hold on for much longer.

The Best Baddie Wins

'Home horrible home,' said Mr Madness.

Demon's legs dropped down and his feet hit solid ground. THUMP! He sighed with relief. As the smoke thinned, he glimpsed orangey-brown rock. They were back inside the volcano at St Viper's.

By the time assembly came around a few days later, everyone already knew the gossip. Demon sat cross-legged in the school hall with the rest of his year, on a concrete island surrounded by a deep channel of blue water. Sharks circled it. He watched the last few boys and girls sprint across a metal bridge over the water. Doctor Super Evil rested a long bony finger on the button that made the bridge collapse.

BANG! A puff of green smoke materialised in front of Demon.

'Guys, do you think Mr Madness ever uses doors?' whispered Stretch.

As expected, the head teacher appeared in front of them, holding a football in one hand and a yellow plastic paint sprayer in the other. Shimmering black liquid sloshed around the inside of a bottle below the nozzle.

Stretch nudged Demon. 'That's kinda how I imagined the invisibility sprayer.'

'A vile morning to you, my venomous vipers,' said Mr Madness in a raised voice.

'HAR, HAR, HAR, HAR, HAR,' everyone cried, in their best evil laugh.

The head teacher jumped to the side to avoid a splash from one of the sharks. 'We're going to start our assembly this morning by talking about the motto of our school. Can any of the First Years please tell me what it is?'

A few pupils in the front row raised their hands, including Shrink.

Mr Madness looked at a boy with mountainous muscles. 'Yes, Bulldozer.'

'May the best baddie win, sir,' he said.

'Thank you.' Mr Madness nodded. 'Our motto sums up the true spirit of St Viper's. It is there to guide us in all we do.' He clasped his blackened hands together and grinned. 'Just recently, I was tickled turquoise to see four First Years living by our motto when they stole a rocket ship from a group of senior students. Demon, Shrink, Stretch and Wolfgang would you stand up, please.'

Demon and his friends jumped to their feet with huge smiles on their faces.

'Dastardly done.' Mr Madness clipped a snake-shaped metal badge onto each of their jumpsuits. 'You are well on your way to becoming super villains. Keep up the bad work.'

The First Years whooped, whistled and cheered, while the senior boys and girls in the back row looked at them with stoney faces.

Demon bubbled over with happiness. His friends looked equally thrilled. Wolfgang ran around in a circle chasing an invisible tail.

'What do you say?' said Mr Madness.

'Thank you,' replied Demon.

Mr Madness rolled his eyes. 'Haven't your parents taught you anything?' Then he mouthed what he expected to hear from them. 'After 3,' he prompted. '1, 2, 3 –'

'Victory is ours!' they shouted together, and all the pupils stamped their feet and clapped.

'Now before you sit down, I need you to help me with an immensely important test. As you all know, hey-hey, the invisibility sprayer is central to our sinister scheme to Take Over The World!' The head teacher threw the football he was holding to Demon. 'When I say "big brown bogey" I want you to throw the ball up into the air and I will spray the special solution on it to make it *invisible*.' Mr Madness planted several kisses along the nozzle. 'Big brown bogey!' he shouted.

Demon hurled the ball into the air, watched Mr Madness spray it, and saw it vanish. He gasped, as did most of the other pupils.

Mr Madness let out an evil laugh. 'MWAHAHAHAHAHA.'

BOK! Demon heard the football bounce near his feet. As he looked at the spot, he noticed a football-sized black circle filled with sparkly dots. It reminded him of the view from the window in the spaceship. He remembered Mr Madness saying that ultra-ordinaries had planned to use the invisible paint on satellites and spaceships to make them undetectable. *It must camouflage objects only in outer space,* he thought.

He noticed Shrink was staring at the same place. 'Let's not be the ones to tell him,' whispered Demon. 'He'll flip.'

The head teacher gestured them back to their places on the floor.

Stretch remained standing. 'Sir, when do we get the reward money back?'

'The school will take complete care of it for you.' Mr Madness pushed on Stretch's shoulders to force her to sit down. 'Such a sum wouldn't be safe left lying around your room, now would it? Not in a school full of super villains!'

The sneaky old teacher is keeping the reward for himself, Demon thought. At that moment, a shark gave a great smack with its tail. SPLASH! An enormous jet of water hit Mr Madness. His two horns drooped like a dog's ears.

Everyone giggled. Mr Madness scrunched up his face and threatened the shark with a fist. But then even he began to chuckle.

'Vhat are ve going to do now?' asked Wolfgang.

'Get that reward back for a start,' replied Demon.

"Then we'll plan for World Domination,' said Stretch, with a wicked smile.

Acknowledgements

I have never had so much support with a novel. Prior to publication, I asked people if they wouldn't mind reading St Viper's and telling me what they thought of it. I hoped a few kind readers might offer to help, but to my surprise nearly three hundred friends, family, children, mums and dads, teachers, on-line reviewers (on Authonomy and Youwriteon), an artist and a designer and other writers came to my aid. I am very touched by their support and grateful for their suggestions and words of encouragement.

Special thanks to:

- Christopher (eight-year-old evil genius). Advisor on comic book super heroes and super villains and number one critic.

- Mark. Fight scenes, sound effects specialist and super husband.

- Anthony. Top illustrator.

- Nick. Graphic designer.

- Victoria. Early draft advisor and coffee drinking buddy.

- Alex. Editor and American language consultant.

- Jenny, Janine and Kay. The best book editors in the world.

www.stvipers.wordpress.com

Demon has his own blog.

Find out about the next book, tell

him (and his writer slave) what you think of

The Riotous Rocket Ship Robbery and join in

with the fun.

He hopes to hear from you soon.

I realy like it becouse
it is realy intresting and
I ~~that~~ thing I will like
it!

Love megan x

Toby

Becky x Chivers x x

Josh

& Ruby

Sam

Walter

to 01225 301989

Darryl

Mausk

Jake

Flop

Angel

Oliver

Barrington

Elive

Arhow Gourit

mr mgta

Tack

Flo

Frederic

Beth

Lightning Source UK Ltd.
Milton Keynes UK
UKOW051600100512

192309UK00001B/5/P